Mrs. Donald's Dog BUN
and His Home Away from Home

by William Maxwell

illustrated by James Stevenson

🐎 Alfred A. Knopf · New York

THIS IS A BORZOI BOOK PUBLISHED BY ALFRED A. KNOPF, INC.

Published in the United States of America by Alfred A. Knopf, Inc., New York, and simultaneously
in Canada by Random House of Canada Limited, Toronto. Distributed by Random House, Inc., New York.

Library of Congress Cataloging-in-Publication Data
Maxwell, William.
Mrs. Donald's dog Bun and his home away from home / by William Maxwell; illustrated by James Stevenson.
p. cm.
Summary: Dr. and Mrs. Donald's dog Bun dreams of living in his own little house instead of the
Donalds' house, but when his wish comes true it is not as nice as he expected.
ISBN 0-679-86053-3 (trade)—ISBN 0-679-96053-8 (lib. bdg.)
[1. Dogs—Fiction. 2. Dwellings—Fiction.] I. Stevenson, James, ill. II. Title.
PZ7.M449Bu 1995
[E]—dc20 93-42390

Manufactured in Singapore
10 9 8 7 6 5 4 3 2 1

For Bun's faithful friend E. G. M.,
without whom this book would be
nowhere

—W. M.

The dog that belonged to Dr. and Mrs. Donald was named Bun, and he was partly Boston bull, partly sheepdog, and partly Labrador retriever, so he was very sensitive to remarks about his appearance.

Although the Donalds lived in a large, comfortable house on a wide street with overhanging trees, and the bones that came from their table were worth waiting for, Bun was not allowed on the beds, or even on the living room sofa, and had to sleep on a musty old piece of carpet in the back hall, where people were always coming and going and saying, "Excuse me, Bun," as they stepped over him.

And he used to dream, with his head resting on his paws, of the little house he would live in someday—a house all his own, free from drafts, and the furniture reflecting his taste, which was toward thick upholstery, rather than Mrs. Donald's. But it was just a dream, and he didn't really expect anything to come of it.

He didn't have to stay with the Donalds, of course. People are always glad to have a good dog around the place, and if he wanted to, he could start out some fine morning and keep going until he found a neighborhood he liked the looks of, and then stop and scratch himself and look lost, and all kinds of people would say, "What a nice dog! Whose doggie are *you*?" and he'd end up with a piece of carpet that wasn't musty and frayed to sleep on, and more steak bones than he could think of places to bury them in. Undoubtedly somewhere in the world there was somebody who would appreciate his finer qualities and not take him so for granted.

On the other hand, the Donalds had raised him from a puppy, and they would miss him, and he couldn't bear the thought of Mrs. Donald standing at the kitchen door when it was time for him to come in, and calling and calling. So he stayed on, year after year. He didn't always bother to cover up his feelings, though, and Mrs. Donald would look at him over the top of her glasses and say, "What's the matter, Bun? Do I bore you?"

One day, a great big truck backed up to the curb, and two men came up the front walk and went inside and started taking all the furniture out of the house.

Bun barked and barked, and when Mrs. Donald stuck her head out
of an upstairs window and told him to be quiet, he thought, Well,
she doesn't know a burglar when she sees one, and he went on
barking, hoping to attract the attention of the police. But then she
came out on the porch, and he heard her giving the men instructions
about where to put things, and it dawned on him at last that they
were moving men.

He followed the truck to the new house and helped the men unload, and then while they went back for more tables and chairs and boxes and beds, he stayed behind and smcllcd thc place over. It was all right.

The new house was larger and more comfortable than the old one, and it was on a nice quiet street, and the trees in the front yard had been there a long time, and there was plenty of room in the rose garden for him to bury bones in, but what interested him most was the little house out in back, behind the big house.

It was made of two upright piano boxes nailed together, and it had obviously been a child's playhouse at some time or other. There was a padlock on the front door, but by putting his paws on the window sill he could look in.

The window hadn't been washed for years and years. He could just barely see through it, and he made out a table and two little chairs, a toy stove, and a doll's tea set, and a rubber ball, and a storybook.

The pictures somebody had cut out of a magazine and tacked up on the wall were not the ones he would have put up, and there were cobwebs in the corners. But in spite of all that, and the general air of neglect, the playhouse had possibilities. It also had a little front porch where, in his mind's eye, he saw himself sitting and enjoying the peace and quiet of a summer evening.

After the Donalds were settled in, and as comfortable as people ever are at first in a new house, which is not very, Bun turned his attention to the little house in the back yard. Much to his surprise, they let him have a free hand with it. The roof leaked, but you don't expect an old place to be in perfect condition. He tore off all the rotting shingles and nailed on good thick tarpaper instead.

Then he painted the shutters blue, and the trim white, and the
porch floor gray, and the inside walls pink, and threw out all the
rubbish that had accumulated over the years, and borrowed a
comfortable rocking chair and a rag rug from the big house, and
hung up pictures of various members of his family, and buried a few
bones around outside, just to make the place seem lived in.

He sat down for a second to scratch himself before calling it a day, and two dogs came along—a cocker spaniel that belonged in the neighborhood and an Airedale Bun had never laid eyes on before. After they had sniffed Bun and he had sniffed them, the cocker spaniel said, "Nice layout you got here," and Bun felt more or less obliged to invite them in.

He told them what the place was like when he first saw it, and about the pictures on the walls, and the cobwebs, and the roof leaking, and he pointed out all the improvements he'd made, and the Airedale said how nice everything was, and made one or two suggestions that Bun didn't think much of, like painting the shutters green instead of blue. When they started to leave, Bun said, "Just drop in any time. I'm nearly always home," which was what Mrs. Donald said.

Next day they were back, with a silly French poodle who kept exclaiming, "Well, all I can say is you've done wonders! There isn't a doghouse in the neighborhood that compares with it, and I've seen them all."

So Bun showed *him* around, and pointed out all the improvements he'd put into the place, and the poodle made one or two suggestions that Bun didn't agree with, such as, for example, that he ought to add a rumpus room.

The spaniel and the Airedale both thought this was a wonderful idea. They talked about it so much that Bun was rather relieved when they left. It was his house, after all, and he liked it just the way it was.

That afternoon, the poodle came back with an Irish terrier and a couple of other dogs of his acquaintance, and while Bun was showing them through and pointing out all the improvements he'd made, the poodle started explaining to the Irish terrier about the rumpus room that Bun was planning to add on to the house, and before Bun could put them right in the matter, the cocker spaniel and the Airedale turned up, with nothing on their minds, especially, except to pay a social call.

That made lots of dogs, and there was something about the Irish terrier that the Airedale just couldn't stand, and the Irish terrier felt the same way about the Airedale, and the first thing Bun knew there was a dogfight going on right there in his own front yard.

The other dogs all commenced to snarl and bark, and Mrs. Donald came running out of the big house with a pail of water. She meant to throw it on the Airedale and the Irish terrier and Bun got soaked instead, but at least it stopped the fight. "Shoo!" she said. "Go on. Get out of here, all of you!" And they did. They knew when they weren't wanted.

But they were also willing to let bygones be bygones, and so when Bun woke up the next morning, he saw the Irish terrier and the Airedale looking at him through the window. He opened the door and let them in, and said he hoped they understood that they were welcome to drop in any time and bring their friends, but that they had to keep the peace—which they agreed to do.

Well, they came and so did the cocker spaniel and the French
poodle, bright and early in the morning, and they stayed until all
hours of the night, and they brought their friends, and their friends
brought *their* friends, and often there were so many dogs scratching
at fleas or gnawing on old steak bones that they'd dug up out of the
rose garden or just sitting and enjoying the peace and quiet of a
summer evening that there wasn't any room whatever on the front
porch, and Bun had to sit out in the yard on a hard bench that he'd
borrowed from the big house when he found his nice, comfortable
rocking chair was always occupied.

In the fall, it wasn't so pleasant on the porch. The cold and rain drove everybody inside, where there really wasn't room for so many dogs, especially since some of them were quite big dogs.

One evening, Bun caught the French poodle looking at him oddly.
He said, "What's the matter, do I bore you?" and the poodle yawned
and said, "Yes, terribly. And so does your little house. Why don't
you tear down that ungainly front porch and extend the living room
out another ten feet so we aren't all on top of one another?"

Bun didn't say anything. His chin settled slowly on his front paws,
he glanced up at the poodle briefly, with one bloodshot eye, and
then he pretended to be asleep.

Late that night, when his guests had all gone home, Bun went out to
the garage. He rummaged around until he found the padlock that
had been on the door of the playhouse when he first saw it, and
then he opened a can of paint, and found a paintbrush that
Dr. Donald had spent a lot of time cleaning, and he made a nice,
neat sign: To Let. Inquire Next Door.

He hung the sign on the doorknob and put the padlock on the door, and then he loped across the lawn to the big house and spent the night on a rubber mat on the back porch.

When Mrs. Donald came down in the morning to start breakfast, he scratched till she let him in.

"Why, Bun!" she exclaimed. "This *is* a surprise. How are you, you dear old fellow? . . . Yes, yes, of course, and we've missed you too, indeed we have! Come in, why don't you?" He let her make over him, and he even sat and watched politely while she lit the gas under the coffeepot, but then he left the kitchen and padded through the house, sniffing as he went.

He was looking for a little back hall that he remembered, just large enough for one dog, and when he found it, there, sure enough, was the piece of carpet. They hadn't thrown it away. His own piece of carpet. He turned around three times and lay down on it, with a great heaving sigh, and in two minutes he was fast asleep and dreaming of rabbits.